TAME THAT CAT!

BY ANNA KOPP

AN UNOFFICIAL

MINECRAFT

STORY FOR EARLY READERS

For my boys, whose love of Minecraft
fuels their love of reading.

This is Steve.

Steve wants a pet cat.
He has to tame an ocelot.

Ocelots are wild cats.
They live in the jungle.

Steve goes to the jungle.

He looks high and low.
Where is an ocelot?

Is there an ocelot here?

Or here?

Steve keeps looking.
He will not give up.

Finally! An ocelot!

Steve holds out a fish.

The ocelot comes closer.

It starts to eat.

It runs away!

But Steve will not give up.
He tries again.

He comes close to the ocelot.

The ocelot sees the fish.

It starts to eat.
It does not run!

Steve tames the ocelot!

Now it is a cat.

Steve takes his new pet home.
He names it Bud.

Steve looks up at the sky.
Night is coming.

Oh no! A creeper!

The creeper sees Bud.

The creeper runs!

Steve cheers!

He loves his new cat.

28808811R00018

Made in the USA
San Bernardino, CA
06 January 2016